AF439459

If Ever I Cease to Love You

By Shawn Bailey

Shawn Bailey

https://shawnhbailey.weebly.com/

If Ever I Cease to Love You

1st Edition

Copyright© January 22, 2018 by Shawn Bailey

Cover Art by SDBailey

All Rights Reserved

Jaded Press

Marrero, USA

on **ANY** website, offering then to the general public offline in any way, or any other method currently known or yet to be invented. Doing so would be depriving authors of their fair royalties and is a violation of international copyright laws and would cause the offender to be subject to fines or imprisonment. Violators will be prosecuted to the fullest extent of the law.

Dedication

Table of Contents

This page intentionally left blank.

Trademarks and Copyrights:

Audubon Zoo – Audubon Nature Institute, New Orleans

Prius: Toyota Company

Café du Monde: New Orleans

Taeyang and G-Dragon – "Good Boy" – 2015

Frankie Valli – "My Eyes Adore You" – 1975

The Meters – "Hey Pocky Way" – 1974

Adele – "Hello" – 2015

Lou Bega – "Mambo Number 5" – 1999

Earth, Wind and Fire – "Reasons" – 1974

Ricky Martin – "Livin La Vida Loca" - 1999

Chapter One

"Are you available for a private party?"

Jacobi Griffin looked up at the sound of a deep voice. The guy attached to it wasn't too bad either. He was about six feet tall, with muscles and wavy black hair. The ice blue eyes gazing down at him made Jacobi feel a bit self-conscious and horny. "That depends on when and where it is or if I need to provide the alcohol or not."

Mr. Tall and Handsome ran an appreciative gaze over him.

Jacobi tried not to blush. Guys were always trying to flirt with him and some of them tried the most outlandish ways of getting his attention. He could not help the way he looked or the way he was built either. His mother ran a dance studio to help support him and his six siblings. His shapely ass and legs and small waist were the product of sixteen years of dance classes and competition.

"My place, tomorrow night and I'll provide the booze. All you have to do is show up."

"Formal or informal?"

"Formal," the great smelling guy answered. "Wear a black uniform and bring an overnight bag."

Jacobi didn't understand the last part. "I'll be staying the night?"

The other guy nodded. "Yes."

Jacobi frowned. *Why does he assume I'm gay or easy?*

"I'm never wrong," the other guy said as if he'd read Jacobi's mind.

Jacobi's heart picked that particular time to skip a beat. "I don't sleep around on the first date."

The guy smirked. "We'll see." He took out his business card and handed it to Jacobi.

Jacobi looked down at it. Winston James, A. P. James Tour Guides and Party Planners. Oh, so that's why Jacobi thought he'd seen him somewhere before. Winston had made commercials for his company. Jacobi continued reading the address. It was in the Garden District near Saint Charles Avenue. "What time?"

"Nine."

Damn, he hoped there weren't any parades still rolling around that time. The Mardi Gras season had just started and it was going to be non-stop partying in New Orleans for the next two weeks.

"Bring swimming trunks," Winston said.

Oh, so it was that kind of party…rich dudes gone wild. "It's February."

"The hot tub and the swimming pool are heated," Winston said. "Though I doubt if you'll be in them very long."

Jacobi scowled. Just because the man was gorgeous did not mean that he could get Jacobi in his bed.

"See you tomorrow, Jacobi."

"How do you know my name?"

Winston pointed to his chest.

Jacobi looked down. "Oh." He had on a nametag. He watched Winston walk away. *Damn, he's fine.*

Seth, the other bartender on call came over. "Do you know who that was you were just talking to?"

"Who is he?"

"That's Winston James. He's family owns most of the Garden District, some hotels, and a tour and hospitality business or so I've heard."

"Is he married?"

"Hell no," Seth said like he'd asked something ridiculous. "Rumor has it that he's the ultimate party animal. What did he want?"

"Directions," Jacobi lied. He kept his personal business private, and it wasn't against the rules for them to take side jobs in their free time.

A crowd of people came up just as Seth returned to his station. The newcomers took up most of the seats at both bars. They were loud and obnoxious and already two sheets to the wind. He sighed. It was going to be a long night since his and Seth's shift had just begun at nine. It was three in the morning when he finally crawled in bed. If Winston James was the type of party animal Seth mentioned who knew when Jacobi would get his next good night sleep.

****

Winston's alarm sounded at noon like he'd set it to do. He had to get up, shower and dress because he had a lot to do before tonight's party. He had people coming in from Maine to have some fun in the Big Easy. Winston's family owned one of the largest hotel chains in the state and it thrived because there was always something going on in town be it a holiday or festival. And they always sought him out to show them a good time. The older he got the less he wanted to be bothered. He'd much rather come home after work, shower and kick back and watch a movie.

Winston got out of bed. After showering he had a bowl of cereal, avocado toast and hot green tea for breakfast. This was followed up with a trip to the gym. He always thought better after a vigorous workout. Today was no exception. He showered again, changed into a suit and went to a meeting with some backers. Then he tried to get home before the revelry started. His brother Martin arrived to hang out until the real guests came.

"Who are you entertaining tonight?" Martin asked as Winston sampled an appetizer.

"Some new clients from Maine. They're in town for Mardi Gras and staying at one of our hotels. They brought a lot of guests with them and they want to party."

"Idiots," Martin said. "I'm surprised you agreed since Mardi Gras is not your favorite holiday."

"That's because tourists come here and tear up the city and then leave."

Martin helped himself to a canapé and poured himself a drink at the bar. "That's how it's always been." He paused. "Who is the lucky guy for the evening?"

"You say that like you know me." Martin was just two years younger than him.

"That's because I do."

"Okay, he's this guy I've had my eye on for a while now. He's a bartender and cute."

Martin sipped his drink. "How cute?"

"So good-looking I can't stop thinking about him. Imagine an angelic face, big hazel eyes, clean-shaven and just the right size to cuddle."

Martin ate the canapé. "He does sound promising. Does he know he's on the menu?"

Winston shrugged. "I kind of hinted when I told him to bring an overnight bag."

Martin gasped and hissed at him. "No wonder you can't keep a lover. What did he say?"

"That he wasn't easy. That's exactly why I'm interested in him. He's a hard worker, just finished college and goes straight home alone at night. He doesn't even drink alcohol."

"Neither do you, anymore," Martin said. "How do you know so much about him?"

"I've followed him a couple of times," Winston admitted. "His boss provided me with the rest of the information."

"Stalk much?" Martin asked playfully.

"No, he gets off pretty late and plenty of people have been getting mugged lately."

"So, you were doing it to make sure he got home safe?" Martin asked.

Winston nodded. "This one might be the one."

Martin nearly choked on his drink. Winston patted him on the back. "You barely know him."

"That's why I hired him to work the party tonight. I plan to get to know him better after it's over. He'll make some great tips and then he'll have stimulating conversation with me."

"What time is this charmer arriving?" Martin asked.

"Nine. The guests should be here by then. He can set up the bar any way he wants to."

"I can't wait to meet him. He must be special if you hired him."

"So, what's up with your life?" Winston asked.

"Nothing much. I've been busy working with Father, and Mother's complaining that she doesn't see you enough."

"I've been busy and besides we work together five days a week." The doorbell rang and Winston went to answer it. The first of his guests began to arrive. He hoped Jacobi would get here soon.

****

The traffic started to thin out as Jacobi drove down Saint Charles Avenue. A red streetcar passed on his left. Its wheels making clacking sounds going over the track, and it made frequent stops along the way. It still managed to catch up with him at the red lights. When he was a child, his mother used to take him and his six other siblings to ride on and to enjoy the route to the university area and the Audubon Zoo.

The GPS directed him to turn right at the next corner. Jacobi followed the instructions. It took him down a couple of blocks into a neighborhood of huge mansions, a Catholic church and a school. He rode up to a brick two-story. There was a valet outside giving directions and parking cars. "I'm the bartender for Mr. James's party."

"There's employee's entrance was on the side," the valet said.

"Thanks." Jacobi drove around the corner, parked, grabbed his bag and got out. Even the side of the historic house was impressive, from its veranda that went around the entire house to the wrought-ironwork and the green plantation shutters. He knocked on the door and a young woman dressed in a gray uniform with a white apron answered.

"May I help you?"

"My name is Jacobi Griffin and I'm the bartender of the evening."

The young woman looked him over. "Yes, please come in. Mr. James is expecting you." She stepped aside and Jacobi entered. "Right this way."

Jacobi followed her past all of the kitchen workers. They all looked up when the two of them walked by. Jacobi waved. The young woman took him to what appeared to be a grand ballroom. The place was huge. He wondered if this was actually Winston's home or did he just use it to entertain. A few guests had already arrived. She showed him to the bar.

"There's a built-in icemaker, and beer on draft. Someone is going to come along to collect the dirty glasses periodically during the evening."

Jacobi stashed his bag under the bar and saw the supplies he would need, along with a large assortment of wines and liquors.

"My name is Darlene. Just call me if you need anything." She pointed to a phone.

"Thank you," Jacobi said.

Darlene left and he opened the bar.

"Welcome to my home."

Jacobi looked up and almost dropped the box of swizzle sticks. Winston James stared down on him, dressed very debonair in a brown suit with a butter-colored turtleneck sweater. There was another guy with him that could pass for Winston's brother.

"Thank you, Mr. James."

"Mr. James?" the other guy asked. "Call him Winston."

"And you are?"

"Martin James, Winston's younger and good-looking brother."

"It's nice to meet you too, Mr. James," Jacobi said.

"What a brilliant smile. How are you at mixing drinks?"

"What would you like?"

"I'll start with a Scotch on the Rocks," Martin said.

Jacobi put his full attention on Winston. "And you?"

"You."

Jacobi lowered his gaze quickly.

Martin chuckled. "Look at that blush."

Jacobi playfully rolled his eyes at both of them. He made Martin his drink.

Martin sampled it. "Delicious."

"You haven't answered me."

"My big brother doesn't drink alcohol," Martin said.

"Me either," Jacobi confessed.

"He drinks sodas."

"Then I have just the thing." He made Jamaican Fruit punch, sans the liquor, and handed it to him.

"Thank you, what is it?"

"Fruit punch."

Winston drank some of it. "Ooh, I like this. I can do this."

Another guy appeared. "I'd like a White Russian."

Jacobi fixed it and handed the man the glass along with a napkin. He tried his drink too. "This is just what I needed and its fixed exactly the way I like it." He put money in the tip jar. "Keep him on the payroll, Winston. A good bartender is hard to find."

"Thank you," Jacobi said.

"I plan never to let him go," Winston said. The three of them walked away.

Jacobi's heart finally settled down. He caught of glimpse of Winston's broad shoulders from the back. The man definitely had his attention.

****

"Oh my God where did you say you found him?" Martin asked Winston later as they watched Jacobi filling drinks from across the room. "Father is going to love him. You know how the man loves his White Russians."

"He works at a club in the French Quarter. I just happen to see him one night when I was there entertaining clients."

"You took your clients to a gay night club?"

"It's not a gay night club, and just because I'm interested in him doesn't mean he's gay."

Martin chuckled. "I'm no expert but I can say with some confidence from that blush that either he is, or he would turn gay for you."

Winston shook his head. "It doesn't work that way."

"I know that," Martin said. "You wouldn't be showing this much interest if he wasn't."

"If he's not, then I have found a great bartender. If he is, he'll be warming my sheets later after I kick all of you out." His party had turned out to be a big success. There was plenty of food and drink and no one was drunk or tearing up the place, yet.

"So, what do you know about him?"

"He's a bartender who doesn't drink alcohol, he's in his mid to late twenties, and he looks good in black."

"Is that all?" Martin asked.

"His name is Jacobi Griffin and he has an amazing smile and alluring hazel eyes."

"So, nothing right?"

"I know that I'm attracted to him and from that blush earlier I think he's at least curious."

"Then you should take the time to get to know him."

"I plan to do just that. I just hope he talks in his sleep."

Martin laughed. "You're incorrigible."

"Look at him. He's easy on the eyes, had that kick ass Southern accent, and his cologne choice has sealed the deal for me."

"He could have a boyfriend."

"Why are you trying to get me to lose interest?" Winston asked.

"You're barely over Oliver and now you're sniffing behind a gorgeous doe-eyed bartender you barely know. I just don't want you to get hurt again."

Winston cleared his throat to get the vision of his evil ex out of his head. "It wasn't all bad with Ollie. We did have some good times."

"He cheated on you and tried to rob you blind," Martin reminded him.

Winston finished his drink. Oliver could have cleaned him out financially if Winston hadn't insisted on a pre-nup early in the relationship. He walked away with what he came there with, plus the cat, and everything Winston had given him as gifts. He had a feeling Jacobi was different. Not everyone was money grubbing and materialistic like Oliver. "It's like riding a horse, once you fall off you have to dust off the dirt and climb back up in the saddle."

"Well, before you bring him home to meet the family do a background check on him."

"I already have," Winston admitted. "The club owner is a friend of mine and he gave me enough information to use. Jacobi is clean. He doesn't even have a jay-walking ticket."

"I knew you weren't going into another relationship head first. He's cute. I'm rooting for you guys."

"Thanks. I think I've found my Mr. Forever."

"Good," Martin said. "Find out if he has a sister."

****

The party ended earlier than Jacobi expected. He'd had all the glasses washed and put away as Winston said goodbye to his guests. All the people here tonight had been very generous with tipping. Jacobi had Winston's share ready by the time he came over to speak with him.

"What is this?" Winston asked.

"Your share of tonight's tips." The man actually chuckled at him. "What's wrong?"

"Those are yours. You did all the work."

"But you provided the liquor," Jacobi argued.

"They were my guests and I was just providing refreshments."

"It's a lot of money," Jacobi said.

"Keep it," Winston said. "Have you eaten?"

Jacobi shook his head. "No."

"I'll have the cook prepare something for us before she leaves. Did you bring your swim suit?"

Jacobi reached down and came up with his overnight bag. It contained his toiletries, his trunks and a change of clothing.

"Good. Let me show you where you can change." Winston walked him out of the ballroom and into the kitchen. Most of the people who were in there earlier had gone, including Darlene. "Jacobi and I will need something light to eat for dinner after we take advantage of the hot tub and swimming pool."

"Yes, Mr. James," the cook said.

They continued to another room. Jacobi spied a hot tub and a pool inside of the mansion.

"It has a shower and a changing room. I'll just have to go check on the food and I'll be back shortly. Just come out and relax after you put on your trunks." He left the room.

Jacobi changed out of his uniform and showered. Easy-listening music played from a stereo system. Winston was there waiting in the hot tub when Jacobi appeared. The man's gaze locked on him and scanned him from head to toe, making Jacobi very nervous. He took real good care of his body, eating right and never drinking or smoking. Other guys had complimented him, but he hoped Winston James didn't find him lacking.

"Wow," Winston said as Jacobi made it to the edge of the pool. "You are more gorgeous than I imagined."

Jacobi climbed up the stairs and joined him in the heated water. Winston had a tray of canapés waiting when he made it over to him. He also had two glasses of what looked like white wine.

"It's grape juice," Winston told him.

"Is that caviar?" Winston nodded, lifted one from the tray and fed it to Jacobi. It tasted a lot saltier than he'd imagined.

"What's wrong?"

"It's salty," Jacobi answered.

"You've never had fish eggs before?"

Jacobi shook his head.

Winston lifted one of the glasses "Here, wash it down."

Jacobi accepted the glass. "Thank you."

"I can't believe you're a bartender who doesn't drink alcohol. How do you know if you've gotten a mixed drink correct?"

"I follow the recipe to the letter. I'm somewhat of a vegetarian too," Jacobi answered.

"Hmm, I'll have to remember that."

"Don't fret about it. You went to a lot of trouble to please me. I just ate it and I don't think a couple of roe will make me fat."

"I don't think so either," Winston said as he plucked a strawberry from the tray. "Are you allergic to these?"

Jacobi shook his head again. "No."

"Open wide."

Jacobi opened his mouth. Winston fed him the strawberry and then stole a kiss while Jacobi chewed. Jacobi swallowed and then opened him mouth to Winston's prying tongue. His cock woke up.

Winston ended the kiss. "That answered one of my questions."

"What question?" Jacobi asked.

"If you're gay."

"Uh, yeah." Jacobi swam away from him so he could calm down his heart. It was beating so fast. He swam back. "What's the other questions?"

"Does he like me? Is he single? Is there a chance he'd let me make love to him?"

"Yes, to the first two questions. No current boyfriend."

"How about the last one?"

Jacobi wiggled out of his swimming trunks and tossed them over the side of the hot tub. "Not usually, but I'll make the exception this time."

Winston moved closer to him and lifted Jacobi partially out of the water. Winston was incredibly strong, holding him with just one arm. He wrapped his legs around Winston's waist and rubbed his body against him. "Do you work out?"

"At least once a week. I'm into bench-pressing, so I think I can handle you."

"Let's go find out," Jacobi said, freeing the man's waist. He swam over to the stairs and climbed out of the water.

"Wait for me," Winston said, swimming toward the edge. He got out too. Moments later Winston's wet trunks joined Jacobi's. The two of them left the pool room.

"Are we alone?" Jacobi asked.

"Yes, everyone is gone, including the cook."

"Good," Jacobi said. "We don't have to hold back."

Chapter Two

Winston couldn't get enough of Jacobi. His lips were soft and full and tasted on mint. He wondered how the rest of him tasted. "Have you been tested?"

Jacobi nodded. "Just recently. Negative."

"Me too," Winston said. He went back to kissing Jacobi, teasing those luscious lips with his tongue and then kissing his chin and his neck. Winston gently pushed Jacobi back on the mattress. He had a nice hairless chest and he'd man-scaped his jock area perfectly.

Winston liked guys who took pride in their appearance and who practiced good hygiene. Martin always complained about how much time he and their youngest brother John took in the bathroom when they all lived in the same house.

Jacobi had a nice-sized circumcised dick. Winston plopped it in his mouth.

"Mmm," Jacobi moaned as Winston began sucking him. Jacobi just didn't lay there like a limp noodle. He rolled his hips and fucked Winston's mouth.

Winston hoped he was just as hot when Winston was buried inside of him. Jacobi hardened quickly as Winston sucked and played with his balls.

"You do that rather well."

Winston stopped and raised his head. "Thanks." He continued, licking the shaft and giving attention to the small area beneath the scrotum.

"Oh my God," Jacobi uttered as Winston got close to the little treasure.

Winston stopped sucking again. "On your knees so I can prepare you." Luckily, they were in his bedroom. He retrieved the lubrication and rubbers from the en suite. He donned the condom first and then soaked his fingers in lube and eased two of them inside of Jacobi. The little hole was much tighter than he expected. Jacobi tensed a little. "Relax. I'm not bragging but I have a big dick and I don't want to tear you." He felt Jacobi relax and then Winston massaged the gland until it softened.

"That feels so good."

"It's just the preamble," Winston said he withdrew his fingers. He moved into position behind Jacobi, gazing down at an ass to die for. He parted the cheeks and put the head of his cock against the opening and pushed forward.

"Oh!" Jacobi shouted.

Winston eased out and drizzled lube on the condom. He tried entry again.

"Fuck, you weren't kidding!"

Winston smirked. He made it in this time. "No, I wasn't. You're tighter than I expected. How many guys have you been with?"

"One," Jacobi answered.

"Recently?"

"No."

Good gracious. He might as well consider himself being Jacobi's first. Jacobi began rocking back on his knees. "Yes, that's it." Winston stopped talking and began humping the glorious rump. The more cock he introduced inside of Jacobi the more the younger man grunted. "You're so nice and warm."

"You're not all the way inside of me, are you?" Jacobi asked.

"No. I don't want to hurt you."

"I want more," Jacobi said.

Winston eased out. "Get on your back." Jacob changed positions and opened his legs. Winston gazed down. His cock had saluted and was dripping pre-cum.

"Do you see something you like?"

Winston nodded. "It's one of those dilemmas that you don't know if you want to suck it or fuck it."

Jacobi spread his legs wider and offered his hole to Winston. "Fuck it."

Winston guided his cock back inside of Jacobi. He thrust forward sending it deep.

"Oh!" Jacobi shouted. After that Jacobi kept Winston's attention by working that ass to bring him pleasure too. He'd closed his eyes and was now moaning softly.

Winston palmed Jacobi's hips and began sliding him bodily to and fro on his rod. Jacobi wet his palm by licking it and then wrapped it around his dick and stroked it. Winston gulped. It was the sexiest thing he'd ever seen. Jacobi reached over and found the tube of lube. He squeezed some into his palm and went back to masturbating.

"Ooh!" Winston said as he fought the impending orgasm.

"Do you like what I'm doing?"

"Hell yes," Winston answered.

"I think I'm about to come."

Winston eased out and then plunged deep.

"Ah!" Jacobi shot cum all over his hand.

Winston fought to keep from coming too soon. He looked away as Jacobi's cock started to shrink and Jacobi rode out the climax.

"I'm a sticky mess."

Winston raised Jacobi's legs and put them against his chest. He eased out to the head and then thrust hard. Jacobi stopped talking and grunted as Winston pumped his hips. "Your ass is so good." The orgasm he'd held back appeared again and Winston knew he was losing the battle. "Get ready. I'm about to come." He started fucking harder and faster. "Oh, oh, ooh!" The cum shot from out of him and into the head of the condom that was buried inside of Jacobi. His body shook as his cock kept spurting. It eventually stopped and Winston lowered Jacobi's legs. "I've never experienced anything so intense." He wiped the sweat from his forehead and away from his eyes with his fingers.

"Me either," Jacobi said he watched Winston recover.

Winston pulled out of him and then they took a short nap. Winston woke up aroused again. He slipped on a clean condom, lubed it up and then he kissed the sleeping Jacobi. Jacobi slowly opened his eyes. "I want you again."

"Okay." He woke up fully and then moved over Winston.

Winston never saw anything so beautiful as Jacobi's descent and the sleepy look on his face. Winston held his cock still as Jacobi spread his cheeks and sat down on the erection.

Jacobi moaned as Winston's dick entered his tender ass. He woke up and began riding Winston's erection. It didn't take long for him to become aroused again. Even sticky with lube and dried on cum it was still the best sight to Winston. He gripped Jacobi by his slim hips and moved him up and down on his rod. "You're the sexiest creature on earth and I want nothing more than to fuck you until you come."

Jacobi continued to ride Winston, moaning and making the cutest little love sounds.

"Let's change positions. I need you on your knees."

Jacobi moved into place and Winston slipped back inside. "This might get a bit intense but I can't help it." He didn't have time to give Jacobi an explanation. He'd never been this turned on before. They got down to some serious fucking as he gave Jacobi every inch of his cock. Jacobi just kept coming until he had nothing left to shoot. Winston felt the moment the orgasm caught up with him too. He wrapped his legs around Jacobi's hips and rode him down to the mattress. Jacobi's screams of passion mixed with his as Winston finally came for the second time. He lay on top on Jacobi for a minute or two and then he lifted his weight off of him easing his deflated dick out. "Are you okay?"

"Yes, but I don't think I'll be able to sit down for a week." Jacobi rolled over on his side as Winston got rid of the condom.

He lay down and Jacobi snuggled up to him. "Where do we go from here?"

"Anywhere you want to," Winston said. "The sky's the limit." All he heard was Jacobi snoring peacefully beside him. Winston sighed. *I can get use to this.*

****

Winston was missing from bed when Jacobi woke. The pleasant aroma of food greeted him as he sat up. An unbelievable pain shot through his ass when he tried to get off of the bed. Jacobi eased back down on the mattress. He'd only been with one guy before but he remembered what it felt like the morning after. He had to soak and he needed some aspirin. Jacobi tried to stand again. He made it successfully into the bathroom and ran some hot water into the tub. Jacobi closed his eyes and soaked for a while and then washed. He got out, dried off and found the aspirin he needed in the medicine cabinet. He dressed after brushing his teeth and washing his face. He found a note from Winston on the pillow when he walked back into the bedroom telling him to come down to breakfast in the kitchen. Jacobi found his way there.

"Good morning," Winston said as Jacob arrived.

"Morning," Jacobi said.

"Have a seat. Breakfast is ready."

Jacobi tried to sit down. "Oh!"

"Hmm, sorry about that. I think I got a bit out of control."

"You think?" Jacobi asked as he eased down into the seat.

"In my defense I'd never been with a guy who I wanted to be with all night and that my cock just loved."

Jacobi never felt so embarrassed in his life.

Winston chuckled. "I love the blush." He sat a plate of food in front of him. "The cook fixed it and left it for us. I let her know that you're a vegetarian. Do you want coffee or tea?"

"Coffee," Jacobi answered.

Winston poured two cups and joined him at the table.

Jacobi helped himself to the cream and sugar and seasoned his coffee. The cook had prepared him a vegetarian omelet, pancakes with butter and syrup and lots of fruit. Channel Six news played on the television Winston had mounted on the wall. Jacobi blessed his food and then sampled it. The pancakes nearly melted in his mouth. "Give my compliments to the chef."

"I'll tell her that you appreciated the effort. Emily comes in twice a day to make sure I don't starve."

"She must have gotten here with the roosters to prepare all of this."

"What can I say? My employees like me."

They continued eating in silence while watching the news.

"So, what do you do when you're not at the club?"

"Sleep," Jacobi answered.

"Hobbies?"

"Reading and collecting manga."

"Really?" Winston asked.

Jacobi nodded. "A hobby from childhood. What about you?"

"Stamp collecting."

Jacobi laughed. "Really?"

Winston nodded this time. "My nana got me into it when I was a kid."

"Nana?"

"My grandmother," Winston said. "She and I used to spend hours together when I was a young. She passed last year."

"Were the two of you still close when you got older?"

"Yes," Winston answered. "I visited her every Sunday after church."

"Oh, you're going to be late for service this morning."

"Relax. I'm allowed to miss one day. Today I'm spending it trying to get to know a very interesting person."

Jacobi cheeks heated from embarrassment. "What do you want to know?"

"Everything," Winston answered. "Do you have any family?"

Jacobi nodded. "I am the youngest of seven children. My parents and grandparents are still alive."

"Six siblings? What do your parents do for a living?"

"My mother runs a dance studio and my father works for the post office."

"Do you dance?"

Jacobi nodded again. "Yes. I took lessons and competed until I graduated from high school."

"Hmmm," Winston said as he sipped his hot coffee. "That would explain that killer ass."

Jacobi rolled his eyes and picked up his cup. "Is that all that you like about me?"

"Are you kidding?" Winston asked. "You're gorgeous and I like talking with you. What part of town did you grow up in?"

"Seventh Ward," Jacobi answered. "I went to Catholic schools. What about you?"

"Both parents are alive, along with my paternal grandfather. I have two younger brothers. You met Martin last night. We have another brother named John. He's four years younger than me."

"No sisters?"

Winston shook his head. "Nope, parents gave up after John. It was a smart move. He's a total brat."

Jacobi chuckled. "You mean he was."

"Nope, he still is."

"So, big brother keeps him in line?"

Winston laughed. "I try, but I think he's a lost cause."

Jacobi liked a guy with a sense of humor. He looked around the kitchen. Everything was state-of-the-art. "So, what do you really do for a living?"

"You didn't read the card?"

Jacobi shook his head. "I just scanned it for your name and address. I think I've forgotten everything else."

"Normally young men would have run a make on me by now to see how much I'm worth."

"This is a very nice home. Is it yours?"

Winston laughed again. "You're a card. Yes, it's mine. So, you're not impressed by money?"

"It's good to have, but it does not influence who I sleep with."

"Hmmm, about that. How old are you?"

"Twenty-six."

"How old were you when you first had sex with a guy?"

"Eighteen," Jacobi answered.

"How old were you when you last had sex with a guy?"

"Eighteen."

"You've never been in serious relationship before?"

Jacobi shook his head.

"What made you take a chance on me?"

"Your cologne."

"My cologne?" Winston answered.

Jacobi smiled and nodded at him. "Yes. I noticed it the first time you came into the club."

"The first time? So, you saw me before the other night when I invited you here?"

Jacobi ate a piece of his pancake and swallowed before he answered. "Yes. You came in a couple of times before then. The first time you were there with several people. Your cologne has a very comforting fragrance. I kept imagining your arms wrapped around me protecting me from all the problems in the world."

"Shit, that's deep," Winston said seriously.

"What made you invite me to be the bartender for your party?"

"I want to say it was your gorgeous face and big hazel eyes, but the fact I chose you because the owner of the club told me you were the best bartender he had."

"My boss?"

"Yeah. He's a friend and I trust his judgment. The fact that you're a babe was an added bonus."

"Do you normally sleep with the hired help?"

"No, Jacobi. And you can believe me on that. I'm very particular with who I share the passion with."

Jacobi went back to eating his food. "You still never answered me about your job."

"Actually, I am an events planner for my family's business, but my diploma says I'm an interior designer."

"Do you like doing what you do?"

"Most of the time," Winston answered. "The people that I entertained last night are guests who've come in for Mardi Gras. They are very rich and mostly all of them complimented me on your bartending skills." He paused. "Do you like doing it?"

Jacobi shrugged. "It helped me pay my way through college."

"Bartending school?"

Jacobi shook his head. "Medical school."

"You're a doctor?"

"An intern. Or I will be next month."

"Then you'll give up being a bartender?"

"That depends on my schedule." Jacobi left right after breakfast. He and Winston promised to get together soon.

****

"How was your evening with the hazel-eyed bartender?" Martin asked.

"What hazel-eyed bartender?" their younger brother asked.

Winston tried to shush Martin. Like him, John preferred the company of men. "This guy I'm dating."

"You're dating someone?" their mother, Amanda, asked as she entered the conference room at A. P. James, Tour Guides and Party Planners.

"I wouldn't exactly call it dating. We've just met." He understood their concern. His breakup with Oliver had almost destroyed him mentally. Since then, he hadn't really dated anyone, just a few one-night stands to take the edge off. "His name is Jacobi Griffin and he's a medical student."

"I thought Martin said he was a bartender," John said.

"He's that too. He's paying his way through college."

"He's a student?" their father William asked. "How old is this guy?"

"Twenty-six," Winston answered. "He's actually an intern."

"Well, at least you've found a date for the Endymion Ball," his mother said.

"I don't know about that yet. I have a feeling he doesn't even like Mardi Gras."

"Isn't he from New Orleans?" his father asked.

"Yes, he grew up in the Seventh Ward."

"What do his parents do?" his mother asked.

"His mother runs a dance studio and his father works for the post office. Jacobi is the youngest of seven children. He has the cute little southern accent and big hazel eyes, and—"

Martin cleared his throat to stop him from giving away too much information to the folks.

"What club does he work at?" John asked.

Winston almost spilled the beans. He wasn't about to lose a guy to his baby brother. "It doesn't matter."

John smirked. "What's wrong? Afraid of a little healthy competition?"

"No, this isn't a game, John. Jacobi is the first guy I've been serious about in a long time."

John rolled his eyes like he didn't believe him.

"Back to this ball thing," his mother said. "Please invite him."

"It's kind of short notice since the ball is next Saturday. He might have to work."

"Ask him," his mother said.

"Okay," Winston said, knowing he couldn't win this argument.

"How did the party go?" his father asked.

"Fine. The Martindales had a ball. They're probably still trying to recover from drinking so much."

"Are they still doing the bar hop after the parade?" his mother asked.

"Yes, they brought a lot of people with them this time and they all like to party."

"Don't let them get too wasted."

"Easier said than done." Bar-hopping meant just that, going from bar to bar drinking the house specialty and dancing up a storm. "I'll make sure they eat something first." The Martindales had spent a tiny fortune on their vacation and the least he could do was feed them.

"What about you two?" their father asked. "Are you working with clients tonight?"

"I'm attending a ball tonight," Martin said.

John answered next. "Guiding a tour."

"What about you guys?" Winston asked his parents.

"We'll be at the country club in Belle Chasse with your grandfather, Adam."

"Oh yeah, I forgot about the geezer ball," John said.

Both parents frowned at his joke.

"Don't call them that," his mother said. "Those senior citizens are some of the richest people in Louisiana, and they like to dance and have fun like you kids."

"I doubt that," John mumbled.

Winston frowned at his problem child. "You just have to have the last word, don't you?"

John shook his head. "No, but I didn't mean anything by calling them that. It was just a joke, of which the parental units have no sense of humor."

The parents ignored John's last remark. "Don't stay out too late," William said to his parents.

"You know how your grandfather is. He's a party animal too."

How well Winston knew this. His grandfather loved to dance and sing and had opened the company sixty years ago so he could show tourists a good time. The business excelled to buying hotels to house their guests and expanding the tour service to include not only New Orleans but some of the other scenic cities in Louisiana too. His grandfather got pretty pissed off at him for not following his father in getting a degree in Hotel and Hospitality. Instead, he'd followed his own heart and studied Interior Design. So far, he was handling both jobs fairly well. And his grandfather hadn't taken him out of the will yet. Surprisingly enough he'd taken Winston being gay better than he took his choice of college majors.

The meeting ended early and Winston went to his office to confirm the bar hop with the Martindales. He texted Jacobi to find out what time he was getting off tonight because his club was the last on the bar-hopping list.

Two in the morning Jacobi texted back.

I might be stopping by a little before that with some people.

I'll be here. There was a pause and then Jacobi continued. *Bring an overnight bag.*

"Yes!" Winston said loudly.

Martin popped in to his door. "Is anything wrong?"

"Second date," Winston answered.

"Congratulations," Martin said. "Don't forget to ask him to be your date for the ball."

"You're worse than mother," Winston said.

"That's why I'm her favorite."

"Only because you're her last hope for getting grandchildren."

"That's not entirely true, but it still doesn't change the fact that I'm the favorite," Martin said. He waved and went back next door to his office.

Winston checked on the furniture delivery for one of his clients. The Edwards had just brought a new house in the Garden District and had hired him to furnish it. Mrs. Edwards liked modern stuff while her husband preferred traditional. He thought he'd done a good showing them pieces that went well together from both types. He picked up his phone again and dialed the delivery service.

"This is Mr. Winston James confirming delivery time for the Edwards' mansion on Saint Charles Avenue. One. Thank you." He disconnected and called Mrs. Edwards and told her that her furniture would be delivered on time. His phone rang as soon as he got off the phone with her. "Yes, this is Winston James. You're in town for Mardi Gras and you and four friends are looking for a good time?" Winston recognized the voice. It was Rocky Monroe a guy he'd dated in college. Rocky, a musician had left New Orleans after Hurricane Katrina and set up shop in Memphis, Tennessee. "What do you have in mind? Sorry, I have a boyfriend. But I do have a barhop beginning in the French Quarter at six pm today if you and your guests want to join us. Where are you staying?" Winston wrote all the information down. "The tour bus driver will pick all of you up between 5:30 and 6:00 pm. We need at least two hours' notice if you change your mind so we can fill the spots. I'll see you then." He disconnected the call. The nerve of some people expecting him to be available after so many years had passed.

The landline phone began ringing non-stop after that. Tourists were rolling into town at the last minute and expecting them to fit them in. For big events like this people usually made reservations a year in advance. If this kept up, he would never get the chance to spend some time with Jacobi. As it was, he was booked solid up until Mardi Gras, Super Sunday and Saint Patrick's Day. He penciled Jacobi in for Valentine's Day. At least he could do was be available for that day. Later that afternoon their receptionist Helen came in. "We have a king cake in the employees' lounge."

"I'm on a diet."

Helen ignored him. "It's your favorite with the white icing on the top and just like the ones that McKenzie' Bakery used to make."

McKenzie's Bakery went out of business when he was a child but he still remembered his mother going there for their king cakes every year. Sweets were still his downfall. "Okay, just a tiny piece." He followed Helen out of the office and down the hall. His brother Martin was in the lounge.

"Someone already got the baby," Martin said.

It was tradition that whoever got the tiny plastic baby in their slice purchased the next king cake. "Who?"

"Me," Martin said, pulling it out of his shirt pocket and showing it to Winston.

Winston fixed himself a cup of coffee and then cut himself a small piece of cake.

"Dieting?" Martin asked.

Winston nodded. "And dating."

"I don't think mon petite bartender would mind a little baby fat on you."

"I'm doing this for me." He'd been a chubby child and they had a cook who knew how to prepare every dessert in existence, including pralines. Over the years Winston had learned to measure his food and to log it into his food diary. When he had a sexy young thing sitting on his lap, he didn't want his belly to get in the way. "And for your information mon petite bartender has a rocking body beneath that uniform."

"I'm so proud of you. You hit a home run."

Winston cleared his throat. "Several. We are very compatible."

"You mean he has a big butt and the two of you partied all night long."

"I was trying not to be graphic," Winston said. "But yeah!"

"Thanks," Martin said. "I like my women with curves too."

Winston ate his cake. He and Martin parted company. Winston went back to his office. The rest of the day went by swiftly. He couldn't wait to see Jacobi again.

Chapter Three

The last parade of the night had finally passed and the crowds of people poured into Paradise Bar and Karaoke Club on Bourbon Street. Mondays were usually slow, except during Carnival time. The club had three bartenders on call, dressed in red and black like the waiters and waitresses. Jacobi spotted Winston and his group around eleven. Winston didn't have a hair out of place, did appear sober and from where Jacobi stood, he looked very handsome in his brown coat, a tan turtleneck sweater and brown slacks.

"I'd like a Scotch on the Rocks."

Jacobi looked at the guy who'd taken the center seat at his bar. He was handsome with black hair and startling blue eyes. Like the other guests he was dressed for the winter in a black coat with a blue sweater that matched his eyes. Jacobi fixed the drink and placed it in front to the guy. Blue eyes paid for his drink.

"Hi, I'm John."

"Jacobi."

"Hello Jacobi. Have you worked here long?"

"About four years." His gaydar went off. "Are you from around here?"

John nodded. "Saint Charles Avenue area. I'm here with friends, saw you and thought I'd introduce myself."

Part of his job was to talk with the patrons. In four years, he thought he'd heard every pick-up line. "Did you check out the parades earlier?" Jacobi asked, changing the subject.

John sampled his drink. "Yes. My friends are from out of town and it is fun to see their reactions to the floats and the costumes and the other tourists. I heard about this place so I brought them here for the food and the karaoke."

The nightly shows always brought in more customers. His boss had come up with the ingenious idea about a year ago. Even though New Orleans was known for the music, some people just had no talent. His ears just got assaulted by drunks and would be pop idols. And the tourists were just as bad. Some came in singing in their native tongue. One of the most popular songs, was G-Dragon and Taeyang's 'Good Boy'. "So, are you going to perform tonight?"

John shook his head. "No, I knowing my limitations, but one of my friends is a great singer. I might be able to coax him into belt out a song or two."

Two guys showed up to his bar and ordered beer. Jacobi carded them before handing over the brew. The guys took the bottles and walked away.

"You thought they were kids?" John asked.

"Yes, I can't be too sure. I wouldn't want my boss to lose his liquor license."

"Do you like being a bartender?"

Jacobi nodded. "It helps pay the bills."

Someone played, 'Hey Pocky Way' by the Meters, and before he knew it people were on the dance floor second-lining. Others were singing at the top of their lungs. The karaoke show started shortly after that. John ordered another drink. "You're cute. Are you dating anyone?"

"Kind of. I just met someone." He hadn't seen Winston in a while, but Jacobi didn't think he'd left.

"I'll be back. I have to go to the little boy's room," John said. He left the bar and his drink.

Jacobi removed it before someone got the idea to spike it. It wasn't unheard of and Jacobi didn't want anything to happen to John. He seemed like a nice enough guy, but at the moment he only had eyes for the gorgeous guy who had found his way to the karaoke stage. Jacobi wondered what Winston was attempting to sing. *Oh my God!* He'd chosen Frankie Valli's 'My Eyes Adored You.' That was his mother's favorite song.

"He's good, isn't he?"

John had returned. "Yes," Jacobi said as he made John a new drink. "Never leave your glass unattended. Someone could drop something nasty in it and you'd wake up on your knees in a strange guy's bed."

"Ooh thanks," John said. "Did that happen to you?"

Jacobi didn't answer him. He went back to listening to Winston sing and trying to get his attention by adding Jacobi's name to the song.

"You know him?" John asked.

Jacobi nodded. "I recently acted as bartender at one of his private parties."

"He comes from a rich family."

"That doesn't interest me," Jacobi said. "He just has the most beautiful eyes and his smile lights up this bar."

"Ooh!" John said again. "You're a romantic."

"I don't know about that. All I know is my heart beats fast whenever he's near. Money is okay, but love is better."

John looked at him oddly. "You're in love with him?"

Jacobi nodded. "Funny, because I just met him. I think about him all the time and I miss him when he's not near me."

A guy came for John. "It was nice talking to you, Jacobi. You have a good night."

"You too, John." John left and another blue-eyed guy took his seat moments later.

"You were wonderful," Jacobi said as he fixed Winston a drink.

"Thanks." Winston sampled it. "Diet soda?"

Jacobi nodded. "I haven't forgotten that you don't drink alcohol and you working out at the gym means you're watching your weight."

Winton gave him a little lopsided smile. "I've been thinking about you all day. I can't wait to get you alone."

"Me too," Jacobi said.

Another guy came up to the bar. This one was blond and a tad bit shorter than Winston. "Oh, this is where you disappeared to, Winston. Aren't you going to buy me a drink?"

"I think you've reached your limit, Rocky."

"But this is the last stop on our agenda, Winston. One more can't hurt me."

"Another one of these for my friend," Winston said to Jacobi. He raised his glass.

Jacobi fixed the guy a diet soda. He was already drunk on his ass so he probably couldn't tell the difference.

"Thanks, Jacobi," Winston said.

"You're welcome. A client?"

Winston nodded. "This is Rocky Monroe."

"The musician?" Jacobi asked. Rocky had aged a lot since the last time Jacobi had seen him perform.

Winston nodded.

"Hello," Rocky said, not taking his eyes off of Winston.

"I like your songs," Jacobi said. "Have you moved back home to New Orleans?"

"No," Rocky answered. "I'm just here to party and to see Winston. He and I are old friends."

Jacobi raised an eyebrow.

Rocky tried to explain. "We used to sing together in a group in college. Then he went legitimate on me. Now I hear you're in the furniture business."

"He's an interior designer," Jacobi said.

Rocky looked at him oddly. "Do you two know each other?"

Jacobi nodded. "Yes, he's, my boyfriend."

Winston's eyebrow arched and then came that incredible smile appeared.

"Oh really?" Rocky asked. "I didn't know, sorry." He moved away from Winston, picked up his glass and then left.

"I hope I didn't ruin business for you by telling him that," Jacobi said as he wiped the bar top with a towel.

Winston placed his big hand over his. "No. So, I'm your boyfriend?"

Jacobi nodded. "If you want to be."

"I'm honored," Winston teased. "Do I get any special perks?"

"You get to come home with me tonight. I usually don't get many visitors. And you get to sing that lovely song to me again. You have a wonderful voice."

"Thank you. I grew up in the church and high school choir, and joined a band in college."

"Why didn't you stay in the group with Rocky?"

"I didn't like the attention," Winston said. "Does he seem happy?"

Jacobi shook his head. "No."

"Interior designing and I are a good fit. I get to express my creativity and when I need a break I party with tourists."

"Did you go to the parades earlier?" Jacobi asked.

"Yes, I watched my clients catch stuff, but you know how it was for me."

"You hate Mardi Gras too, don't you?" Jacobi asked.

"I don't exactly hate it, but there is a part of it I do like."

"Like what?"

"Mardi Gras balls," Winston answered.

"I've never been to one or rode on a float," Jacobi confessed. "But I've always wanted to go to Endymion's ball."

"Why that one?"

"Dude, the double-decker floats are amazing," Jacobi said happily.

"What stopped you?"

"I never got invited."

"Would you like to go this year?" Winston asked.

Jacobi stopped rubbing the counter. "What?" It was hard to hear over the karaoke singing.

"Would you like to be my date?"

Jacobi thought about it. "That's this Saturday, isn't it?"

"Yes, do you have to work?"

Jacobi shook his head. "I took off so I could watch the parade on television."

"Then say yes and come with me and see it in person. The floats are going to roll right through the convention center."

Jacobi found himself smiling broadly. "Okay."

"It's formal."

The smile disappeared. "I hope it's not too late to rent a tuxedo."

Winston pretended shock. "You don't own a tuxedo?"

"Do I look like a tuxedo person?" Jacobi asked.

"No, you look like my boyfriend," Winston said. "I better get back to my clients before they ask for a refund." He finished his drink. "I'll meet you at your place later."

"I haven't given you the address."

Winston chuckled. "I've done my homework. I'll have to get these people back to their hotel safely, and then I'm yours for the rest of the night to do whatever you like."

Jacobi smiled at him. "Don't tempt me. I'll see you later."

Winston left and Jacobi went back to work mixing drinks for the revelers.

****

Jacobi lived in a very expensive Vieux Carré apartment. It was a Creole neighborhood in the French Quarter and very close to where he worked. It was on a secluded little cul de sac that offered rare off-street parking for the tenants and their guests. The security at the gate had his name on a list. There was no way Jacobi could afford this on a bartender's salary. Winston parked next to Jacobi's Prius and got out. He reached for his overnight bag and garment bag from the back seat and armed his security alarm. He entered a gate and walked through a courtyard decorated with gardenias and magnolia bushes and trees. The walkway led to some stairs that Winston had to climb. He knocked on the door. Jacobi answered a few minutes later. "You're right on time. Dinner is ready."

"Is it okay if we have dinner later?" Winston asked as he got a whiff of the freshly showered bartender. His damp dark brown hair curled softly around his face.

"Okay." Jacobi let him in, took his hand and escorted him to the bedroom after he locked the door.

Winston didn't remember how the rest of the apartment looked. Adele's 'Hello' blared from the radio. Winston had just enough time to put his things on the back of a chair before he got attacked by Jacobi. The other guy pushed him down in the chair, hopped on his lap and began kissing him.

"I want you in me now."

Easier said than done. Had Jacobi been a female it would have been a matter of just shoving the panties aside and entering. With a guy it took a little bit of ingenuity. He got Jacobi out of his shirt and then got him off his lap and out of his pants and briefs. "On the bed." It was a good thing that he carried condoms in his wallet.

"There's lube in the night table drawer," Jacobi said, rolling over and getting on his knees.

Winston never got undressed so quickly before. He liked do a little strip tease for his date first. Apparently, he didn't need that tactic with Jacobi.

"I'm so hot," Jacobi said.

"Indeed." Jacobi was literally melting the gel that Winston was trying to prepare him with. "What's come over you?"

"Some guy sang this beautiful love song to me earlier," Jacobi said. "I'm a sucker for stuff like that. It turns me on."

"That was hours ago," Winston reminded him.

"Yes, I know. I've been counting the minutes until you arrived."

Winston got the condom on and moved into position behind Jacobi. He put his dick against the hole and Jacobi surprised him by impaling himself before Winston could thrust.

Jacobi moaned loudly. "Oh, you feel so good in me."

This was going to be a quick one. Winston took control away from Jacobi and began fucking him.

"It's so close, Winston. I can feel it."

Winston believed him. Jacobi rocked back and forth on him, taking more of Winston hard cock inside of him. Winston started thrusting to help Jacobi come. It took a little while longer than he expected, like Jacobi was holding back. Jacobi worked his body faster. Winston thrust harder and deeper.

"Yes, that's it," Jacobi said. "I want all of it in me. Make me yours."

Winston didn't know what had gotten into Jacobi, but he liked it. He pumped his hips.

"Ah here it comes. Oh, oh, fuck Winston, this feels so good. I'm yours. Ah!"

Winston felt the hole tighten and vibrate as Jacobi came. He slowed his roll while Jacobi recuperated. "You feel better now?"

"Yes," Jacobi said breathlessly.

Winston eased out and put Jacobi on his back. He went down on him, licking him clean and then moving into position between his legs and sinking into that nice hot butt again. This time he took control going in and out of Jacobi slowly until Jacobi got aroused again. Jacobi's next orgasm was just as intense as the first one. But this time Winston witnessed it firsthand. Winston had raised Jacobi's legs against his chest and he was now working his dick in and out of the tight hole.

"Oh my God!" Jacobi shouted as he spurted cum all over his pubes. Some of it oozed out of the little slit in his dick head.

The sight proved too much for Winston. He rocked his hips faster and then he started humping Jacobi. "Hold on I'm about to blow. Oh, ah, yeah!" he shouted as he came.

Jacobi put his legs down. Winston stayed in place a few seconds and then eased out of him. He took off the soiled condom and tossed it into the waste can next to the nightstand. He lay down and pulled Jacobi to him to cuddle.

Jacobi pressed his sweat-damp head into the crook of Winston's arms. "I'm spent."

"Me too."

"I'll see you in the morning."

Winston planted a kiss aside Jacobi's head as sleep over took him too. "I'll be here."

****

Jacobi was missing from the bed when Winston woke up, but the pillow next to him still had the indention where Jacobi's head had been. Delicious aromas filled the room. Winston stretched and sat up. Jacobi had opened the curtain and the sun shined through. He looked around. Jacobi had a nice big bedroom and a king-sized. There was a dresser and chest of drawers and beautiful artwork on the walls. The comforter on the bed was brown and gold and matched the print on the chairs. Winston got off the bed. His clothing had been picked up and folded neatly on the seat of the chair Jacobi had attacked him in. Winston smiled remembering what had happened. He got his overnight bag and headed into the bathroom. Jacobi had left him towels. There were male toiletries, cosmetics and skin care medication on the counter, and one lone toothbrush in the holder. Winston showered and dried off, and snooped a little more while he brushed his teeth and washed his face. Jacobi had scented candles and bath bombs in his cabinet. He put on his underwear and a robe Jacobi had left him and his slippers and went in search of his lover. He found Jacobi seated at the table watching the Channel Six morning news. "Anything interesting going on?"

Jacobi tore his gaze away from the screen. "No parades scheduled for today. It's going to be cold and there aren't any traffic jams around town." He ran his gaze over Winston. "You look so good in a robe and slippers."

"Thanks, you still have some guy's robe here?"

Jacobi shook his head. "Someone gave it to me as a gift. It was too big for me. I'm glad I kept it. It fits you perfectly. Sit down, I made breakfast."

"You know how to cook?"

Jacobi nodded. "I was the youngest of seven kids so I spent a lot of time in the kitchen with my mother as she prepared breakfast for us."

Winston sat down and Jacobi got up and dished up two plates of food.

"I have wheat toast."

"That's the best kind," Winston said. Moments later Jacobi placed the food before him…grits, hash brown, scrambled eggs and toast. Someone was going to work out very hard at the gym later.

"Do you like orange or grape juice?"

"Orange," Winston answered.

"Coffee or tea?"

"Coffee."

Jacobi finally joined him at the table. He blessed his food.

"Did you sleep okay?"

"Yes. I don't know when I slept so peacefully," Jacobi admitted. "What about you?"

"Your bed is very comfortable." Winston began eating his grits. They had just the right amount of butter and salt, and the hash browns melted on his tongue. Jacobi Griffin was a very good cook. He never met a guy who knew his way around the kitchen. "Do you have to work today?"

"Tonight," Jacobi answered. "I have to be there at seven. What about you?"

That meant Jacobi wouldn't get off until around three in the morning.

"Tour group."

"That sounds interesting," Jacobi said playfully.

"That's because you live in the area. Tourists love this stuff. Would you like to join us? I'll have you back in time for work."

"Sure," Jacobi said. "Only if you have dinner with me."

"Oh, yeah, we missed eating last night."

Jacobi nodded. "It's a date. What should I wear?"

"Nothing fancy," Winston said. "It's going to be cold, so make sure you bundle up. Wear comfortable shoes too, because it's a walking tour."

"Okay, it sounds like fun," Jacobi said. "I better go see if I can order a tuxedo too. Any color preference?"

"Black," Winston said. "White gets dirty very easily."

After breakfast Winston got a tour of the place. It had two bedrooms, a living room, a bath and a half and a kitchen. It also had plenty of closets, which was rare in the French Quarter, a charming fireplace and a great view of the neighborhood. And it was immaculately clean and had to cost Jacobi a pretty penny to upkeep. It wasn't cluttered either.

"I'm not materialistic," Jacobi explained. "The apartment was a graduation gift for myself. I've been saving for it a long time."

It was in a perfect location and Winston understood how much Jacobi had to sacrifice to afford it.

They eventually got dressed, even though Winston wouldn't have minded another romp on the sheets with Jacobi.

"We'll have a lifetime to be intimate, but only a short time to bring a little happiness to tourists."

Winston nodded and the two of them parted ways. He drove back home and then went to the office. He'd meet up with Jacobi later when he joined his tour group.

****

Seeing New Orleans through the eyes of out-of-towners was more fun than Jacobi had anticipated. He had only agreed to go just to spend more time with Winston. Jacobi knew they had only known each other a short time, but something inside of him told him that Winston was the guy he was destined to spend the rest of his life with. The main problem was that they were from two completely different worlds, and they both worked strange hours. Before he jumped in head first he wanted to get to know Winston better.

"Are you wearing enough?" Winston asked Jacobi as he fixed his collar. He zipped up Jacobi's coat to make sure he had enough protection from the bitter cold at his chest.

"Yes," Jacobi answered as he let Winston treat him like a baby. He had on a scarf, and a knit hat and gloves. Winston looked fantastic in a full-length navy-blue wool coat, a scarf and a hat. Winston had the height and the physique to look good in anything he wore.

The tour began right on time in front to the James's Canal Street Hotel. Everyone had on a red glow in the dark bracelet that had the hotel's name and address on it in the event they got lost. Winston escorted his group near the aquarium and down Decatur Street. Jacobi listened as Winston told the tourists about the history of the French Quarter. They actually stopped and ate beignets at Café du Monde and then they visited the two museums in the area. No trip would be complete without visiting the little shops near the St. Louis Cathedral. The area was also known for its entertainment…fortune tellers, artists and living statues. Freelance musicians also could be found sitting on the sidewalks playing songs for tourists for a price. Winston spun the tales of Jean Lafitte the pirate and Marie Laveau, the voodoo priestess as the tour made its way through the heart of the Quarter. Winston was a very good story-teller and quite knowledgeable about the city. Jacobi noticed the way Winston stayed away from the French Market. He was responsible for a big group of people and he probably didn't want to lose any of them to the large fruit and flea market. They eventually made it over to Bourbon Street. Jacobi waved goodbye to Winston and turned the corner and entered the employee's entrance to the club where he worked. He changed into his uniform, set up his bar and began his workday. He texted Winston later thanking him for the lovely evening. He kind of expected Winston to show up when Jacobi got off at one in the morning. Jacobi had left his car parked at work earlier and walked over and met Winston's tour, so he didn't need a ride home. The tour must have tuckered Winston out because Winston didn't return his text. Jacobi fixed himself something to eat after he showered. It was almost five in the morning when he crawled into bed. He planned to catch up on some much-needed sleep.

Chapter Four

"You look very delicious in a tuxedo," Winston said looking down on Jacobi as they stood in Jacobi's foyer.

"You mean handsome," Jacobi said as he grabbed his overnight bag and suit bag and left out of the door. Winston followed him. Jacobi handed the stuff to Winston so he could lock the door.

"No, I mean delicious," Winston said as they walked to his car. He put Jacobi's stuff in the back seat and the two of them got into the front.

Jacobi put on the seatbelt. He tried to keep his tux from getting wrinkled. "You look delicious in a tux too, and debonair."

Winston chuckled. "I wasn't fishing for a compliment. You really look good in that color."

Instead of choosing a black or white tuxedo, Jacobi went for the charcoal gray. He'd gotten a haircut and a close shave earlier that day. He hoped Winston appreciated the effort. "Thanks. Your cologne smells heavenly." All Jacobi wanted to do was snuggled up next to him and inhaled the scent all night. It might sound freaky, but that's what came to his mind.

"Look at all the traffic," Winston said as they made their way to the convention center where the ball was being held.

"Parking is going to be a bear," Jacobi said.

"I have a spot," Winston said.

"You own a spot at the convention center?"

Winston shook his head. "No, I reserved one a block away. I don't do anything half-assed." He parked the car and the two of them got out.

Jacobi smoothed the wrinkles out of his jacket as they crossed the street and walked to their assigned entrance door. There were people everywhere. He and Winston finally made it inside.

"We need to find our table."

It didn't matter where they sat, they still would not be close enough to the main stage. Everything would be broadcasted over the many large screens throughout the hall. Several women gave him and Winston more than just a passing glance as they walked by them.

"You draw a lot of attention," Winston said.

"They're looking at you," Jacobi told them. "They probably think I'm your pesky baby brother or something."

Winston chuckled. "No, you're nothing like my pesky baby brother. Ah, there's our table."

Jacobi followed Winston over to it. It was filled with men and women elegantly dressed in tuxedos and ball gowns. He couldn't help but noticed that most of them were checking him out. The venue itself was huge and all the tables were filled with food and alcohol. Their table was manned by a caterer. Jacobi sat down next to Winston. Several minutes later the first of the superfloats arrived. Jacobi caught so much stuff he didn't know what he was going to do with it.

The Mardi Gras Indians entered later after the band performing on stage stopped playing. They brought along their own brass band to entertain the audience. People hopped to their feet to do the second-line, twirling small umbrellas and blowing whistles as the Indians sang several Carnival songs and danced. Their costume featured every color of the rainbow. Like the float makers, the members of the tribes started working on their suits the day after Fat Tuesday.

Winston handed him a glass.

"What's this?"

"Non-alcoholic champagne."

Jacobi sampled his. "The good stuff," he said. Winston excused himself to use the men's room. Jacobi watched him walk away. He looked good from the back too.

"Ah, fancy meeting you here."

Jacobi recognized the voice. He looked up to find John, the guy from the karaoke night seated in the chair Winston had exited.

"Care to dance?"

"I can't. I'm with my date."

John looked around. "Oh, you mean the guy you arrived with?"

Jacobi nodded.

"I'm sure he won't mind."

"I rather not test him," Jacobi said.

John chuckled. "I thought you were joking about dating someone until I saw the two of you come in together."

"Why would you assume I was joking?"

"I thought you just said that to get rid of me."

Jacobi saw Winston heading back in his direction. He got stopped by a group of people. There was a lot of hand-shaking and back patting.

"Those are some of his friends," John explained. "The one on the right is Henry Forrester. He and Winston have been buddies since elementary school. The one next to him is Ernest Johnson. He and Winston played high school football on the same team."

"You seem to know a lot about Winston."

"I rather know more about you," John said. "I can show you a better time than him. Why date an old guy when you can have someone your age to hang out with."

"Winston isn't old," Jacobi said.

"He's thirty-five."

"And sexy," Jacobi replied as Winston looked his way.

"What's so sexy about him?" John asked.

"Are you kidding me?" Jacobi asked. "Look at him. He's tall, muscular, and handsome and has that banging body."

"And he's rich."

"Not an issue," Jacobi said. "He's eloquent."

John laughed. "He's been called a lot of things, but never that. What else?"

"Seeing him makes my heart beat and my pulse race."

"I can make you scream my name while you come."

Jacobi unconsciously took his attention off Winston and put them on John. "Your brother would kill me and you both."

John chuckled. "When did you figure out who I am?"

"Just tonight. I remembered him telling me that he had a younger bratty brother named John. And you guys do resemble. I just didn't know you were…"

"Pitching for the other team?"

"Yeah," Jacobi said.

"He called me bratty?"

Jacobi nodded.

"My parents would like to meet you," John said.

"They're here?"

John nodded. "The entire family is here seated at the table. Didn't Winston tell you?"

"No, no wonder it felt like everyone was checking me out when Winston and I came in."

"Don't worry. I think you made a great first impression. You look damn good in that tuxedo. You'll get to meet everyone at breakfast after the ball." He sighed. "Winston is so damn lucky. I wished I had found you first."

"Hmmm, do you pitch for the team or are you a catcher?"

"Both," John answered. "Keep me in mind if you ever decide to drop my brother."

Jacobi turned up his nose. Never in a million year would he ever consider dating brothers.

Winston returned to the table. "Is he bothering you?"

Jacobi shook his head. "No, John and I were just getting to know each other."

"Can I dance with him?" John asked."

"That is completely up to him," Winston said looking down on Jacobi.

"I bet he can't dance," John said. "No one is that perfect."

Someone played Lou Bega's 'Mambo Number Five.'

"I'm about to find out," Winston said. He took Jacobi's hand and dragged him to the dance floor.

Jacobi danced circles around Winston, though Winston had a good grasp of the mambo too. Others joined them for Ricky Martin's 'Living La Vida Loca.' "For an old guy, as your brother calls you, you have some pretty smooth moves."

"I'm going to kill him," Winston said.

"Can't. Got to love the baby. He's cute and I think he idolizes you," Jacobi said as Winston swing-danced him across the floor. Others cheered them on.

"You're very good," Winston said. He swung Jacobi under his leg and hopped over him.

"You too," Jacobi said as they both faced each other. That song ended and a slow one played.

Winston pulled Jacobi into his arms. Both of their hearts were beating fast from the previous dance. "Now this is the kind of music I like."

Jacobi knew the song. It was Earth, Wind and Fire's 'Reason.' He remembered the lady next door to them playing it over and over again when he was a kid. A lot of people always annihilated the song on karaoke night.

"You don't seem a bit freaked out dancing with another guy in front of all of these people."

"Should I be?" Jacobi asked.

"No," Winston said. "There's nothing wrong with dancing with your boyfriend."

Chapter Five

"Mom and Pop, I'd like you to meet Jacobi Griffin, my boyfriend." Winston hadn't brought anyone home to meet the folks since the Oliver fiasco. He pushed Jacobi forward.

"It's nice to meet you," Jacobi said.

"You can go, Winston," his mother said. "Dad and I would like to get to know your young man."

Jacobi looked surprised but not terrified. He sat down in the parlor between the seats where Winston's parents were seated.

Martin led Winston away. "They won't eat him. Let's give them time to get to know him."

Winston smiled at Jacobi and left the parlor and went to visit with his other family members. It was five in the morning and normally he and Jacobi would be asleep by now. But he didn't want to break tradition. Every year his family ate breakfast together after the Endymion ball.

John appeared. "You are so lucky."

Winston ruffled the thirty-year-old's hair like he used to do to him as a kid.

John pushed his hand away. "I'm not a child anymore."

"Stay away from my boyfriend," Winston said.

"I'm beginning to think that there's something wrong with him," John said as the three of them ended up in the dining room.

"What do you mean?" Martin asked.

John continued to fix his hair. "I think he likes the big goon."

"Why would you say that?" Winston asked. "What did he say?"

"Something soppy and romantic about you making his heart and pulse race whenever he sees you or something like that."

Winston smiled. "He said that?"

John nodded. "He also didn't fall for my best line."

"What best line?" Martin asked.

"I promised I'd rock his world in bed." Both he and Martin laughed. "What's so funny?"

Winston answered him. "No offense, but I've already rocked his world and his planet. Jacobi is mine, that is, if the folks don't scare him off."

His cousin Beatrice walked in. "Breakfast is ready, and sorry John, but I think your mother is ready to adopt Jacobi. Did you see him dance at the ball? She's already plotting to get him to be her ballroom dancing partner at the country club."

Martin gave Winston a thumb up. The rest of the family began arriving. Beatrice left and returned with the cook carting in food. Jacobi sat next to Winston's mother. Winston sat down across from him. John sat on the other side of Jacobi. Both Martin and John had dates at the ball but they weren't there for breakfast. They probably took them home so they wouldn't be drooling over Jacobi. Winston winked at Jacobi. Jacobi blushed. John was checking both of them out.

"We can use a doctor in the family," their mother said to her husband.

"We can use a good bartender too," his father said.

Every now and then Winston saw Jacobi steal looks at him.

"You two are perfect for each other," Martin said. "You guys looked great on the dance floor."

"How many years of dancing have you had?" William's mother Amanda asked.

"Sixteen years," Jacobi answered. "I started at the age of two. My mother owns a dance school and studio."

"That would answer a lot of questions," Martin said. "Now if he could cook he would be the total package."

Winston coughed, cleared his throat and winked at Jacobi once he got his attention.

John leaned toward him. "Can you cook?"

Jacobi nodded.

"Do you have a brother?"

"Four of them," Jacobi answered. "I can't wait to introduce you to them."

Winston sighed. His family liked Jacobi. Proper courting had officially begun.

****

Thank God he didn't have to be at work until six that evening because he hadn't woken up until three on Sunday afternoon. He would have to go straight to work from Winston's place. Luckily, he had a clean uniform in his locker. Winston sat at the other side of the room at a desk doing paperwork. He had showered and dressed and looked hard at work. "Why didn't you wake me?"

"Because we didn't get in until seven this morning."

Jacobi groaned. "Don't remind me. I'll make it up tonight. I have to return my tuxedo."

"I've done that already when I returned mine. I'll bring you to your place to get your car so you won't be late for work."

Jacobi went into the bathroom, showered and headed back to the bedroom to dress. Winston had left a note for him to join him in the kitchen. Jacobi still couldn't get over how large the house was. He could get around in it better now and he didn't get lost quite as often.

"Emily made lunch. It's egg salad."

"Did you tell her that I was a vegetarian?"

Winston nodded.

"You don't have to be."

"This body needs some pampering. I don't need meat to survive on."

Jacobi sat down and Winston served him. They cheated by eating potato chips with their sandwiches. Jacobi's phone rang. It was his mother. He put her on speaker. "Hello?"

"Junie Bug, it's Mama."

Winston smirked at him like he'd just learned a secret.

"Hi Mama. What's up?"

"That's what I'd like to know. We haven't heard from you in a while."

"I'm still working nights and sleeping my days away. How's Daddy?"

"He's fine. He hasn't heard from you either. Drake said you must be dating." Drake was the brother next to him.

"He's right. I have met someone."

"Is he a nice guy?"

"Yes, Mama. His name is Winston James and he's sitting across from me at the table listening to my conversation."

"Hello Winston."

"Hello, Mrs. Griffin. Junie Bug is off tomorrow so I'll make sure he comes to dinner to see you and Mr. Griffin."

Jacobi made a face at Winston.

"You come too," Mrs. Griffin said. "If you're dating him then we expect to meet you."

"Yes, ma'am."

"Junie I hope you're eating right. Winston, my Junie's a good cook but he won't eat anything that isn't nutritious."

"And who fault is that?" Jacobi asked playfully. "A dancer has to keep his or her weight under control."

"You're not competing anymore," his mother reminded him. "You were always my best student. Did you watch your favorite parade on television last night?"

"Better than that Mama, Winston and I went to the ball, and the floats passed right through the convention center."

"Thanks Winston," his mother said. "I like you already. Dinner will be served at seven. I'll see you two then."

"I'll have him there on time," Winston said.

"See you later, Mama. I have to get to work."

"Oh, okay Junie. I love you."

"I love you too. See you tomorrow." Jacobi pressed the speaker button. Winston was chuckling. "Don't you dare."

"How can I resist, Junie Bug?"

"Drake couldn't say, Jacobi. He called me Junie and it stuck."

"I think it's cute."

"I think I better warn you that the rest of my siblings might put in an appearance for dinner."

"Bring them on. I have two jobs, own my home and car and no police record."

"They're a lot to take at one time," Jacobi warned.

"I'm not afraid," Winston said. As promised, Winston dropped Jacobi off at home.

****

Winston changed into a suit and then went to meet with his new clients, the Moores. They were recently married and wanted something different than the stuffy old French provincial furniture they had inherited from Richard's grandmother. Beth and Richard were both successful lawyers and could afford his fees. Afterward he went home again to meet up with clients who wanted to go to the Bacchus parade. He got quite a delightful surprise when a very sleepy Junie Bug buzzed his phone at three in the morning.

"I can't sleep."

"Where are you?" Winston asked.

"At your front door."

Winston hurried down and looked into the peephole as a precaution. Then he opened the door. Jacobi smelled freshly showered and shampooed. In fact, his hair was still damp and he had on a pair of jogging pants and a T-shirt. "Come on in here before you catch pneumonia. Are you hungry?"

Jacobi entered and shook his head. "No, sleepy." He took Winston's hand and led him out of the foyer and up the stairs to Winston's room. He stripped and climbed into Winston's bed. Winston tried to get back in his spot. "Take your clothes off first."

Winston stripped and crawled back into the spot he had deserted earlier. Jacobi cuddled up next to him. Jacobi went to sleep. Though flattered, Winston would lecture his younger lover in the morning about the evils of driving while exhausted. Jacobi snuggled up closer to him, snoring peacefully. Winston sighed and closed his eyes. *I can get very used to this.*

****

Once again it was near noon when Jacobi opened his eyes. It was like dating a vampire. Winston had already eaten breakfast, made several business calls before Jacobi decided to join the land of the living. "Good afternoon."

Jacobi groaned. "What time is it?"

"Almost lunch time," Winston answered.

Jacobi sat up, yawned and stretched. The covers moved down to his waist. "Oh naked."

"Very," Winston said watching him from the other side of the room.

Jacobi got off the bed and pulled the jogging pants on over the best ass in the world. He grabbed his toiletry kit and headed into Winston's bathroom. He returned later, showered, shaved and smelling wonderful. He was still bare-chested and showing a lot of skin.

"Are you hungry?"

"Starving," Jacobi said as he tugged his T-shirt down over his body, ending Winston's peepshow.

"Did you sleep well?"

Jacobi nodded.

"Next time call and I'll come for you, or I'll send my driver to get you. You shouldn't drive sleepy."

"Sorry for waking you up too."

"No need to apologize. In fact, I'm flattered that you think I have a comfortable bed."

"It's not the bed."

"No?"

Jacobi shook his head and pointed at him.

"Oh, is it that you like sleeping next to me?" The blush to Jacobi's cheeks was instantaneously. He'd never been in a situation before that someone actually liked him and not just his money. "I like sleeping next to you too."

They headed to the kitchen. Winston figured he wouldn't be able to wake Jacobi until late so he asked his cook Emily to prepare both of them something light for lunch. She fixed tomato soup, a salad and meatless lasagna for them. "So, what tired you out so much?"

"A huge crowd came in after the Bacchus parade. There were a lot of college guys. You know the type, football frat guys with big egos, big thirsts and no self-control."

"Yes, been there, was one of them,"

"All three bars were busy. And it was all you can eat hot wings night, and you know there's no such thing when it comes to these guys. They don't buy mixed drinks, it's strictly beer with them and I had to keep changing kegs because they drank us dry."

Winston tried to keep from laughing. "Did you make a lot of tips?"

Jacobi stared at him. "No, they are the worst type of patron. They're cheap and they don't tip."

"I'll make sure I'll give you a big tip the next time I come into the club."

"That will have to wait. I won't be going back there for few days."

"You're on vacation."

"Sort of," Jacobi said.

"How long do you have off?"

"A week," Jacobi answered. "The club is going through renovations."

"What are your plans?"

"Sleep."

"Come to Gulfport with me."

"What?"

"We have a hotel there. We can go there and be obnoxious tourists."

"What will your folks say?"

Winston pulled out his cell phone and punched in some numbers. "Mom, it's me Winston." He turned on the speaker. "Would it be okay if I take Jacobi on a little trip to Gulfport since he's off for the next few days? We want to be obnoxious tourists at one of our hotels."

"Fine. While you're there check to see if they need anything. You two have fun."

"Thanks Mom." He hung up and dialed another number. "This is Mr. Winston James. I'd like to book the ambassador suite for tomorrow through check out Saturday morning. Yes, I realized tomorrow is Mardi Gras. We own the hotel, remember, oh yeah, that Mr. Winston James. I'm bringing a guest. Also schedule us for all the shows and free reign with room service and the buffet. Yes, my mother knows. You can call her." The clerk took the challenge. A few minutes later he returned to the phone.

"She said to put you in the honeymoon suite and hopefully you'll make a grandchild."

Talk about Jacobi turning many shades of red. "Okay, wise guy. My sweety and I will be in around eleven tomorrow. We'll see you tomorrow." He hung up.

"Your mother did not say that."

"Yes, she did," Winston said. "I can't wait to meet your family."

****

Negotiating around New Orleans on Lundy Gras...the Monday before Mardi Gras, wasn't an easy task. Streets were still marked and blocked off for the arrival of Zulu and the Rex royalty. Jacobi's folks now lived in Gentilly. They pulled up to a two-story home with a nice front porch and a big yard and got out.

Jacobi knocked on the door. Seconds later an older woman answered. "It's Junie Bug," she said to someone. "Come on in." The house was newly furnished and had a scent of seafood in the air. Something other than Jacobi smelled delicious.

"Mama, this is Winston James. Winston this is my mother, Francis."

She and Jacobi resembled each other. Winston shook the woman's hand. "It's nice to meet you, Mrs. Griffin."

"Oh, you're just gorgeous," she said. "Now I see why Junie hasn't been visiting lately."

Winston chuckled. "Thanks for the compliment. These are for you?" He gave her the flowers he'd purchased on the way there. It wasn't easy to find a florist open on Lundi Gras.

"Thank you, they're beautiful." She invited them inside and he and Jacobi followed her through the house to the dining room.

Jacobi had not exaggerated; he had a big family. "Everyone this is Winston James, Junie's boyfriend."

Winston expected a frown at least from one of them. None.

"This is Junie's father, Robert."

Winston walked over and shook the older man's hand. "It's nice to meet you, Mr. Griffin."

The man shook his hand. "Call me Bob, everyone does." The older guy still had a head full of hair. Jacobi would probably have his until he was that age or older. He did resemble his father. He had dark hair too, but brown eyes.

Francis continued the introduction. "These are the Junie's older brothers, Robert, Jr., Austin, Stanley and Drake, and his sisters, Ava and Ana."

The twins. Jacobi had mentioned them. Drake appeared a little older than Jacobi, had brown hair, but green eyes. He also had a nice shape like his younger brother. "It's nice to meet all of you." He and Jacobi sat down. The questions began right after the food got blessed.

"How did the two of you meet?" Bob asked.

"I saw him when I brought in some clients for a few drinks,"

"How did you know that he was…special?"

"The word is gay, dad," Drake said. "Wait, he is special too."

The other brothers laughed at his joke.

"Very funny," Jacobi said.

"Was it love at first sight?" Ava asked.

"It was for me," Winston said.

"What does your family do?" Robert, Jr. asked.

"We're in the tourist business," Winston answered. "My grandfather owns A. P. James, Tour Guides and Party Planners."

"I knew you looked familiar," Francis said. "You were in a commercial with your grandfather when you were a boy."

"Wow, you have a very good memory. That was nearly thirty years ago."

"She can remember all seven of the kids' names," Bob said. "I just call them son. All the girls answer too."

Winston smiled. Bob had a great sense of humor.

"Nearly thirty years ago?" Drake said. "Dude how old are you?"

"Thirty-five," Winston answered. "I was just about to turn five when I made that commercial with my grandfather."

"That would make Junie…"

"One lucky bottom," Jacobi said happily. He even chuckled wickedly.

"See, I told you he was special," Drake said.

"And gorgeous," Winston added.

"So, you work for your grandfather," Stanley said. "In what capacity?"

"I, my three brothers and our parents, arrange tours for tourists."

"Is there much money in it?" Stanley asked.

"He's the accountant, isn't he?"

Jacobi nodded.

"Junie won't starve if that's what you're asking."

Jacobi bragged a little. "He has a cook named, Emily. She fixes me lunch."

"Your parents have a cook?" Ava asked.

"Yes, but Emily is mine."

"Oh, that means you have your own place," Ana said.

"Yes. I own my own home."

"Do your parents know that you date guys?" Drake asked.

"Yes," Winston answered. "I came out of the closet when I was fifteen. It was a complete waste of time since they told me they already knew. Apparently having too many toiletries and taking too many bubbly baths is a sure sign that you're gay."

Everyone at the table laughed.

Jacobi was trying not to smile.

"Junie has a ton of toiletries and cosmetics," Drake teased.

"You do too," Junie argued back.

Winston raised an eyebrow. *Oh, so Drake liked guys too.*

"It makes the family interesting," Bob said as if reading his mind.

"My parents met Jacobi on Saturday night," Winston said.

Austin had been quiet most of the time. "You took Junie home to meet your parents? This must be serious."

"About as serious as me meeting his," Winston said. "In fact, we all went to the Endymion ball together.

"Junie was your date?" Ava asked excitedly.

"Yes," Jacobi answered. "We even danced to Mama's song."

"Mambo Number Five?" Drake asked.

Jacobi nodded. "Winston's a good dancer."

"Better than us?" Drake asked.

"No fair," Winston said. "You guys took lessons."

"I sense a challenge," Robert, Jr. said to Austin.

After dinner the Griffins took Winston to their den and had a good old-fashioned dance contest.

"When are you going to quit that night job?" Francis asked Jacobi as he and Winston were about to leave.

"Soon," Jacobi answered. "I'm sure my internship will take up most of my nights."

"Oh, I forgot to tell you. I'm taking Jacobi to Gulfport tomorrow. My family owns a hotel there and both of us can use a break."

"How long will you be gone?" Bob asked.

"Until Saturday afternoon," Jacobi said. "The club is being redecorated. It's like the first and last real vacation I'll have a chance to get from them."

"Be safe," Francis said.

"I'll call you when I get back," Jacobi promised.

He and Winston walked to the car, got in and drove away.

"So, what do you think of them?"

"You have a great family," Winston said. "Is Drake the one you want to introduce John too?"

Jacobi shook his head. "Austin."

"You mean?"

Jacobi nodded. "He's kinda of quiet but he came out to me at the same time I came out to him. He's a nice guy and he needs someone like John to get him out of his shell."

"He is a great looking guy. I'll invite both of them to dinner at my place and then we can see if they click."

****

Jacobi hadn't been to Gulfport in a long time and he never stayed at one of the hotels. The James Hotel wasn't on a ship, but an actual land-based one. The honeymoon suite overlooked the beach and the Gulf of Mexico. It came equipped with a kitchen, a living room and televisions. There were also two desks, computer hookups and lots of clean towels. They found a complimentary bottle of non-alcoholic champagne, snacks and a cheese and cracker tray. "Your idea?" Jacobi asked.

"I called back and had them remove the real champagne," Winston admitted.

"This place is fantastic," Jacobi said.

"You should see the casino and the gym. There's also a spa and we're scheduled for massages after breakfast."

They had left New Orleans very early to avoid all of the Mardi Gras traffic, so they hadn't had time to eat. A few minutes later someone knocked at the door. Jacobi went to answer it. "Who is it?"

"Room service," a male voice answered.

Winston entered the living room. "I took the liberty of ordering before we got on the road."

"Thank you," Jacobi said, suddenly realizing he was now dating a very thoughtful man. The waiter rolled in the cart and set the food on the table in the kitchen. Jacobi made coffee while Winston tipped the waiter.

"Just put the cart with the empty plates outside the room when you finish and I'll come back for them later," the waiter said and left.

Winston had uncovered all of the plates before Jacobi came to the table with their coffee. "I see meat. I'm glad you took my advice."

"It's just a little piece of ham," Winston said.

"Good. You don't have to change your diet because of me, but I appreciate the effort." They both sat down. Besides the ham there were omelets, hash browns, wheat toast and plenty of fresh fruit. It wasn't the greatest food he'd ever eaten, but it killed his hunger. "So, what's on the agenda for today?"

"First our massages and then the grand tour of the hotel."

"You are serious about the spa date?" Jacobi asked.

Winston nodded. "We're on vacation."

"I've never been on a vacation before," Jacobi admitted.

"The rules are very simple," Winston explained. "Just relax and allow yourself to be pampered."

****

A good-looking guy massaging his muscles got no complaints from Winston. He'd had massages before, but this guy knew what he was doing. By the time he finished Winston was feeling no pain. He and Jacobi met up in the spa's waiting area. Jacobi looked a bit more relaxed too. They ended up at a juice bar for a healthy treat. "Are you enjoying yourself?" Winston asked as they went for a walk along the beach a little while later.

"Yes," Jacobi answered. "I would probably be home dozing off while watching the parades if I'd turn down your kind offer." He paused. "How about you?"

"If I were home, I'd be unconscious on the sofa with the parades watching me."

Jacobi yawned. "Speaking of sleep, I could use a nap."

Winston walked him back to the room. "I'm going down to the manager to see how things are going and to check to see if they need anything. You enjoy your nap." He left Jacobi and had a nice meeting with Louis Green. They both went through the inventory and Winston faxed a supply list back to the home office. It was late afternoon when he returned to the room. He found Jacobi still asleep, naked and covered just by some sheets. Winston tiptoed past him, took a quick shower and then joined him in bed.

Jacobi automatically rolled in his direction, snuggled close to him and embedded his face into Winston's side. "Welcome back."

Winston moved Jacobi into the crook of his arm. "Thanks, how was your nap?"

"Relaxing." He eased away from Winston and got out of bed.

Winston watched him walk to the bathroom, heard him relieve his bladder and then wash his hands before returning to the bedroom. He crawled back into bed.

"Did you take care of those things for your mother?"

"Yes, so you have my full attention of the rest of the evening."

"Okay." He lifted the cover. "You're naked."

"Yes. Ooh, wait." Too late. Jacobi had plopped Winston's cock in his mouth and was giving him a great blowjob. Winston tossed back the covers so he could watch.

Jacobi lifted his gaze and stared at him with those intense hazel eyes. He lowered them and continued sucking and licking until Winston's cock grew hard with desire. Winston had planned to take a nap, but this was much more interesting. "Ooh, that feels so good."

Jacobi stroked the length of Winston's shaft and then reached lower and manipulated the balls with his fingers. He gave each a gently squeeze and then hefted them in his palm. Jacobi lowered his head a bit after freeing Winston's cock and gave some attention to Winston scrotum…and beneath it where he was seriously sensitive. Jacobi must have sensed it too because he used his tongue to tease it.

"You keep that up and the ballgame will be over early."

Jacobi chuckled wickedly as he put his attention back on the dick and deep-throated it.

"Oh my God that feels so good. Baby, that is some special skill you have."

Jacobi squeezed Winston's cock harder and began jerking him off while simultaneously sucking the head.

"Wait. Oh!" Winston came sending his deposit down Jacobi's throat.

Jacobi lifted his head and swallowed for Winston to see. "Yummy." He got off the bed and went back into the en suite and brushed his teeth and gargled.

Winston closed his eyes to enjoy the afterglow alone. Jacobi hadn't completely drained him, but he'd weakened him a bit.

His love returned and climbed into the bed with him. "What's next on the agenda?"

"Dinner, a show, dancing and there's a casino here. Do you gamble?"

Jacobi shook his head. "Not really. I stay away from the tables and just play the slots."

"You ever win any big money?"

Jacobi shook his head again. "No. I never play to win. I just play for fun. And besides, these places are tourist traps. What about you?"

"I play the slots some times, but poker is my game."

"You ever win big money?"

Winston nodded. "Yes, sometimes."

"I'll come up to the room and watch some television so I won't distract you while you play. Don't feel that you have to entertain me twenty-four-seven."

"I don't know. Maybe I'll come back to the room to rock your world the rest of the night after I play a few hands," Winston bragged.

Jacobi chuckled. "I'm serious, Winston. This is your vacation too. I brought along my e-reader."

"We'll see. Get back under the covers."

Jacobi moved in next to Winston and snuggled against him. "Ah, do we really need to go to the dining room right now?"

"Why, what's wrong? Aren't you hungry?"

Jacobi pressed his lower body into Winston's hip.

Winston cleared his throat. "Oh. Do you want me to take care of that?"

"If you don't mind," Jacobi said happily. "I wouldn't want to go to dining room with this. It might get too much attention."

"Gladly," Winston said. He dived beneath the covers and went down on him.

Jacobi threw the sheets back. "Oh, baby yeah."

Winston had no problem servicing the hazel-eyed beauty. Plus, his cock had hardened again too and he wanted to bury it into something warm.

Jacobi moaned loudly as Winston tightened his grip around the base of his dick. He used his fingers to stroke and gently massaged the shaft and balls while giving him a fantastic blowjob. Jacobi moved his hips in a circular motion and sent more cock down Winston's throat. "I need you in me Winston!"

Winston released him and Jacobi assumed the position on his knees. Winston wasted no time preparing him; he spat on his fingers and slid them into Jacobi's ass.

"Ooh, that feels wonderful."

"Don't you dare come," Winston warned.

Jacobi chuckled wickedly again. "Then you better put something bigger and better in there."

Winston removed his fingers, put on a condom and then eased his cock into Jacobi's inviting hole.

Jacobi steadied himself and then rocked back and forth on his knees. "You feel so good inside of me, but don't treat me so tenderly. I need it harder."

Winston moved his hips faster to give it to Jacobi the way he wanted. Jacobi just didn't lay there, he kept up that rocking while clenching Winston tightly. Normally Winston could last a good long time before he climaxed, but that was not the case today because his lover was just too damn sexy. He humped faster.

"Don't you dare come before me," Jacobi said, using Winston's own words. "I'm so close."

"I can't make any promises," Winston said. "Your ass is just too good."

Jacobi rolled his hips and sent that fantastic ass into his lower stomach and pelvic region. "Oh, Winton I think I'm about to come."

"Let me help you with that." Winston withdrew to the head and sent the entire length into Jacobi.

Jacobi used a pillow to muffle his screams of passion as he came.

Winston followed him over the edge. "Oh!" He was buried up to his balls in Jacobi and shooting cum into the head of the condom. "Your ass is the bomb."

Jacobi chuckles were muffled by the pillow too. He turned his head a little so he could speak. "Just remember that. I'm yours just as long as you want me."

Winston eased out and rolled off of Jacobi. "What if I want you forever?"

Jacobi turned over. "Are you serious?"

"Yes," Winston said. "I knew from first glance that you were the guy for me."

"That can be arranged," Jacobi said. "Though you might have to share me with a hospital and patients. Sometimes I might be on call for days."

Winston pulled him closer. "I understand that it's a part of the total Jacobi Griffin package. I can live with being the lover of a doctor. Just as long as you understand that sometimes my job takes me out of town, like a trip here and to Texas every now and then. And there's some late nights involved too."

"I understand." Jacobi snuggled up next to Winston. "We can make this work."

"It would work better if you moved in with me."

Jacobi stopped snuggling. "Ooh, where did that come from? Are you serious?"

"I'm very serious, Jacobi. I've been thinking about it since the morning I woke up next to you in bed."

"What about my place?"

"You can still keep it. It's close to the hospital and we can use it on weekends as a place to crash when we work late and can't get back to the Garden District."

"This is a big step, Winston. I wouldn't want to cramp your style or get in the way."

"You won't be getting in the way. The mansion is huge and I get lonely sometimes. You don't have to rush into making a decision right now." Winston heard a tiny snore. Jacobi had fallen asleep. He was getting used to his new partner's sleeping habits. Besides being a bottom had to be exhausting. Winston dozed off too but woke up later, showered, dressed and waited for Jacobi to return to the land of the living. Later the two of them went down to the buffet where they ate seafood gumbo, Alaskan King crab legs and a salad. They watched a show in the hotel… a tribute to the songs of the 70s which Jacobi actually liked it. Next Winston took him dancing at a gay club not too far from the hotel that Winston often frequented whenever he was in town. Maybe they should have stuck to the hotel. The last person he expected to see was his ex-Oliver.

Chapter Six

Jacobi had been having one heck of a time with Winston. They had just sat down after dancing when this guy came over to their table and sat down. He was a little older than Jacobi, with blond hair and blue eyes. He was fashionably dressed in a brown suit cut to fit his petite frame. The arched eyebrows and stylish hair added to his good looks. "Hello Winston."

Winston's entire demeanor changed when he looked up and saw him. "What are you doing here?"

"The same thing you are. I came here with my friends to dance."

"I thought you were in New York with your man of the hour."

"Ah, about him. That's over. I came home because I missed New Orleans and you."

"This isn't New Orleans," Winston reminded him.

"Yes, but your family does own a hotel here so I knew you would eventually show up. Seriously I'm not stalking you. My friends did come here to escape Mardi Gras and enjoy the coast." He looked over at Jacobi. "Hello. I'm Oliver Thomas, and you are?"

"Jacobi Griffin," Winston said. "My boyfriend."

The little light went out of Oliver's eyes with that last announcement. Jacobi did not feel sorry for the guy. Winston had told him all about Oliver and how he'd broken Winston's heart. The nerve of some guys. Did he think he would be able to waltz back into Winston life after what he'd done?

Oliver ran his gaze over him. "Isn't he a bit young, Winston?"

Winston smiled at Jacobi. "Nope, just right. He's a doctor and my parents adore him."

Oliver's smile faltered. "How are they?"

"They're fine, now."

"I miss them, even John."

"You should have thought about that before you did what you did?"

Oliver faced Winston. "I've changed."

"I doubt that. Anyway, it's too late. Jacobi and I are very happy together."

Oliver turned back to Jacobi. "Winston and I were engaged."

"Were," Jacobi said. "He told me everything. You hurt him deeply."

"It wasn't all my fault," Oliver protested. "He hardly had time for me. I don't know how many nights I waited for him to come home."

"It's his job," Jacobi said. "I understand that. I work late hours too, but Winston is still my top priority. On the nights we can't be together we call just to say, goodnight. Part of being in a relationship is compromise."

"You just don't know what it's like to be thrown aside because his clients were more important."

"Then why would you want him back?" Jacobi asked. "His job hasn't changed." Oliver moved around a bit in his chair. Jacobi knew what that meant. He meant he missed having sex with Winston. "Oh yes, he is good at that, but as he mentioned before he's my boyfriend now."

"You don't know what it likes to get tossed aside because his clients are more important. He'd going to do the same to you."

"Maybe," Jacobi said. "But I know how to entertain myself. I don't need Winston's attention twenty-four-seven. I have my own friends and family, and I don't mind snuggling up in his big bed and going to sleep until he comes home."

"He's mine," Oliver said angrily.

Jacobi rolled his eyes. "Winston isn't a possession. What's wrong? Did the money he gave you run out? The bank's closed, honey. We need it for our future kids." He winked at Winston.

Winston faced him. "We're having kids?"

Jacobi nodded. "I promised your parents, first a boy and then a girl."

"His parents adore me," Oliver said.

Jacobi never had to deal with ex-lover drama before, but Oliver was pretty pathetic in his efforts to win Winston back. "I love Winton and he loves me."

"You love me?" Winston asked. The smile on his face lit up the ballroom.

"Yeah. I'll show you how much later."

Oliver chuckled sarcastically. "He'll never be home and you'll be stuck with a mansion full of bratty kids."

"I have six brothers and sisters, plus I'm looking forward to hanging with Winston's grandfather and learning about the family business as well as Winston's other interests."

"I bet you didn't know he's really an interior decorator," Oliver said like that would win him some brownie points.

"Yes, I do know that. He has exquisite tastes and he's mine."

"You just said he wasn't a possession."

"Not yours, mine. You've lost Oliver."

Oliver stood up. "We'll see." He stormed away angrily.

"Sorry about that," Winston said.

"Did you know he was going to be here?" Jacobi asked.

Winston shook his head. "But he probably anticipated I'd come to Gulfport since I don't like the Mardi Gras crowd. He and I used to come here from time to time to dance."

"Then there's nothing to apologize for."

"How did you know I wouldn't fall for him again?"

Jacobi chuckled triumphantly. "Your eyes never left mine."

Winston kept up the questions. "Did you mean it when you said that you loved me?"

Jacobi nodded. "I don't have to lie. I have been in love with you since you kissed me in the hot tub that first night."

"Oh, you mean the time your swimming trunks ended up off you and on the floor in the pool room? That's when I got a glimpse of that spectacular physique. I said damn, he's rocking that ass."

Jacobi nearly fell off his chair laughing. "You're so silly. I've never done anything so brazen before."

"I love you too, Jacobi."

Jacobi stopped laughing. "You do?"

Winston nodded. "Oliver is my past. He and I had some good times, but he's selfish. So far, I don't see that in you. That night you not only offered me your body but your soul too. You're so sexy that I get off just by seeing you come."

Jacobi looked around the make sure no one was listening to Winston's wonderful confession.

"I'd be honored to have babies with you even though I don't know how we're going to accomplish this. I can't make any promises that I won't leave you alone some nights, but I'll try to spend a lot of time with you too."

"Me too. Although I shouldn't make that promise until I find out my schedule at the hospital. We might have to sneak over to my condo for some quickies."

"I'm down with that, Jacobi. How soon can you move in? I love watching you sleep in my bed."

"You watch me while I sleep?"

Winston nodded. "You look like an angel snuggling the pillow."

"Soon," Jacobi said. Someone played the second-line. Jacobi hopped out of his seat and held out his hand. "Let's show these guys how it's done." He didn't like Mardi Gras, but he loved its music.

****

"You are so lucky," John said as he ate some of the chicken and andouille sausage gumbo Jacobi had prepared for dinner. "Not only is Jacobi a doctor but he can dance and cook."

"I can cook," Austin said to John.

John glanced over at him. "Can you dance?"

Austin nodded. "And I think you and I can make beautiful music together."

Jacobi tried not to smile as his older brother came out of his shell to woo Winston's gorgeous younger brother.

"You are pretty charming for a lawyer. I think my parents will agree that you would make a great addition should I succumb to those sexy green eyes and allow you to date me."

Austin laughed. "I like a guy with a great sense of humor. I would love to meet your family and spend some time with you."

Jacobi raised his fist triumphantly. "Yes." He knew the two of them would be a good match. He left them and went to get the main dish, pot roast and potatoes.

"What's your specialty in the kitchen?" John asked Austin.

"Sweets," Austin answered as he served John some pot roast. "Homemade pies and cakes."

"I like sweets," John confessed.

Austin never took his eyes off John. Being gay hadn't been easy for him. Austin was the shy type who would never consider dating John unless he trusted him. "What are you doing later?"

"Going out on a date with you," John answered. "I know the perfect place where we can dance and get to know each other."

"Where?" Austin asked.

"My place," John answered.

Jacobi noted that John was not one to beat around the bush. The two of them finished dinner and left before tasting Jacobi's coconut cake.

"I think they like each other," Winston said as he and Jacobi sat in the hot tub. He had his eyes closed, relaxing.

"Um hum. I wouldn't be surprised if they don't announce their engagement before the year is up."

"Is that a hint?" Winston asked as he moved his hand between Jacobi's legs. "If I ask you to marry me today would you accept?"

"Of course," Jacobi said, enjoying the feel of Winton's fingers gently stroking his cock. "I love you and I want to spend the rest of my life with you. Oh!" The moan slipped from his lips. He heard a click which made him open his eyes. Jacobi stared down at the most exquisite male gold ring inside a black velvet jeweler's box. "What's this?"

"An engagement ring," Winston said as he kept his other hand busy beneath the water. "Jacobi Griffin will you marry me?"

"Um hmm," Jacobi uttered as his cock grew from Winston's touch. "Yes, I'll marry you. He accepted the ring, took it out of the box and tried it on. "It fits perfectly."

Winston's hand moved faster.

"Ooh, sweet Jesus. I think we need to resume this in the bedroom." They made it as far as one of the guest bedrooms downstairs. Jacobi refused to ask why there was lube and condoms in the nightstand. What happened between Winston and some other guy before they met was none of his business. He didn't need much foreplay. His cock was hard from Winston prepping him in the hot tub. "Oh!" He came dripping cum on the sheets.

"Don't fret, I'll get you hard again," Winston promised. The man never let up, pounding his thick dick in Jacobi's ass until he made good on his promise. He made Jacobi lay on his back and then he entered him again. This time he had Jacobi's legs up against his stomach and was slowly moving his cock in and out of him. Jacobi's prick slowly hardened. "You're so sexy."

Jacobi opened his eyes. Winston was over him balancing his weight with his hands pressed against the mattress on both sides of Jacobi. The sight of all those muscles flexing turned Jacobi on. "Make me come again."

Winston spread him wide and then thrust deep into his ass. The force made the bed shake beneath them. Winston picked up the momentum, thrusting and humping while Jacobi moaned passionately from the unbelievable sensations running through him. His cock throbbed. The orgasm was so near the surface he had to keep it from erupting too soon. He moved his legs down from Winston's chest and wrapped them around his waist. He sank down on Winston's dick.

"Open wide, Jacobi. Here comes a big surprise." He swept the sweat from his forehead and then palmed Jacobi's waist and moved him bodily up and down on his shaft. "Oh Lord!" He came deep inside of Jacobi's ass.

Jacobi came again too from Winston rubbing that big cock against the gland in his ass. Winston simply rocked his world in and out of the bedroom.

****

Jacobi admired his ring as he and Winston soaked in the tub in Winston's bedroom. Winston had literally carried him up there and put him in the warm water after sexing him up like no man had ever done before.

"Do you like it?"

Jacobi nodded. "Yes. When do you want to do this?"

"How about we wait until after you finish medical school? That way you can concentrate on getting good grades instead of planning a wedding."

Jacobi agreed with him. "Good idea. That will also give our families time to get to know each other. But I wouldn't be surprised if John and Austin beat us to the altar."

"But they just met?" William said.

"Technically we did too. I didn't say it would happen tomorrow, but Austin is old-fashioned and romantic. I can see him sweeping John off his feet with flowers and candy."

"And the babies?"

Jacobi chuckled. "After the wedding and we're both stable in our careers."

"Don't try to wiggle out of your promise. I want to fill the mansion with kids."

Jacobi yawned. "I won't break the promise."

"I better let you get some rest." Winston climbed out of the tub, dried off and then held open a big bath towel for Jacobi. Afterward they crawled into Winston's bed.

Jacobi snuggled against him, inhaling his manly scent and feeling so loved and protected. "Good night, Winston. I love you."

Winston kissed him. "I love you too, Jacobi. Pleasant dreams."

The End